TOO MANY CARROTS

Katy Hudson

PICTURE WINDOW BOOKS
a capstone imprint

Published by Picture Window Books,
a Capstone imprint
1710 Roe Crest Drive
North Mankato, Minnesota 56003

www.mycapstone.com

Copyright © 2019 by Katy Hudson

For information regarding permissions, write to Capstone, 1710 Roe Crest Drive, North Mankato, MN 56003.

Library of Congress Cataloging-in-Publication data is available on the Library of Congress website.

Summary: Rabbit refuses to give up his carrots, which leads to disaster after disaster. Will friendships be ruined during the carrot chaos?

ISBN: 978-1-5158-3003-0 (paperback)

Designer: K. Fraser

CARROT

To Do:
- Eat carrots
- Plant carrots
- Collect carrots
- Eat carrots

CARROT DIARIES

THE Complete GUIDE TO GROWING CARROTS

CARROT RECIPES

AN ODE TO THE CARROT

Carrot desserts

Carrot POETRY

BEST IN SHOW

KEEP CALM AND CARROT ON

 CARROT

CARROT

CARROT

CARROT

PRORERTY OF RABBIT

CARROT

CARROT

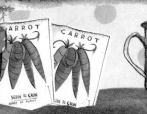

I CAR

Rabbit LOVED carrots!

He collected them wherever he went.

Rabbit was proud of his collection
and burrowed it away in his cozy hole.

But Rabbit had a problem. A BIG problem.

He couldn't sleep!

His cozy hole was too crowded to live in.

"I need a place to sleep," Rabbit told Tortoise.

"You could share my house," Tortoise offered.

"It looks cozy and snug," Rabbit said.

"Maybe it's a little TOO snug for two?" suggested Tortoise.

"Not at all," said Rabbit.

"Oh, dear. Well, perhaps we can stay in Bird's nest," said Rabbit.

"My nest is quite small, Rabbit," said Bird.

"I'm sure we will all fit," replied Rabbit.

Rabbit hauled all his carrots up the tree.

"WHOA!" groaned Tortoise
and Bird as the branch wobbled
and swayed . . .

. . . and SNAPPED!

CRASH!

"I'm so sorry, Bird. Now THREE of us don't have a place to sleep," said Rabbit.

"You can sleep in my house," offered Squirrel.

"Oh, thank you, Squirrel! How kind of you," said Rabbit.

"I don't think any more carrots will fit, Rabbit," said Squirrel.

"Just a few more," Rabbit replied.

"Uh-oh," whimpered Tortoise, Bird, and Squirrel.

"Now FOUR of us don't have anywhere
to sleep," grumbled Squirrel.

"You can sleep at my house," called Beaver.
"It has plenty of space."

"Great! I can bring even more carrots,"
Rabbit said with a smile.

"But with all your carrots we can't fit inside,"
said Beaver, a bit bewildered.

Just then, the rain started. Tortoise shivered.
Bird whimpered. Squirrel squeaked.

And Beaver heard a TERRIBLE rumble as his house collapsed.

"Oh, no! My house!" yelled Beaver.

"Oh, no! My carrots!" cried Rabbit.

"Ahh

hhhhhhhhhh!”

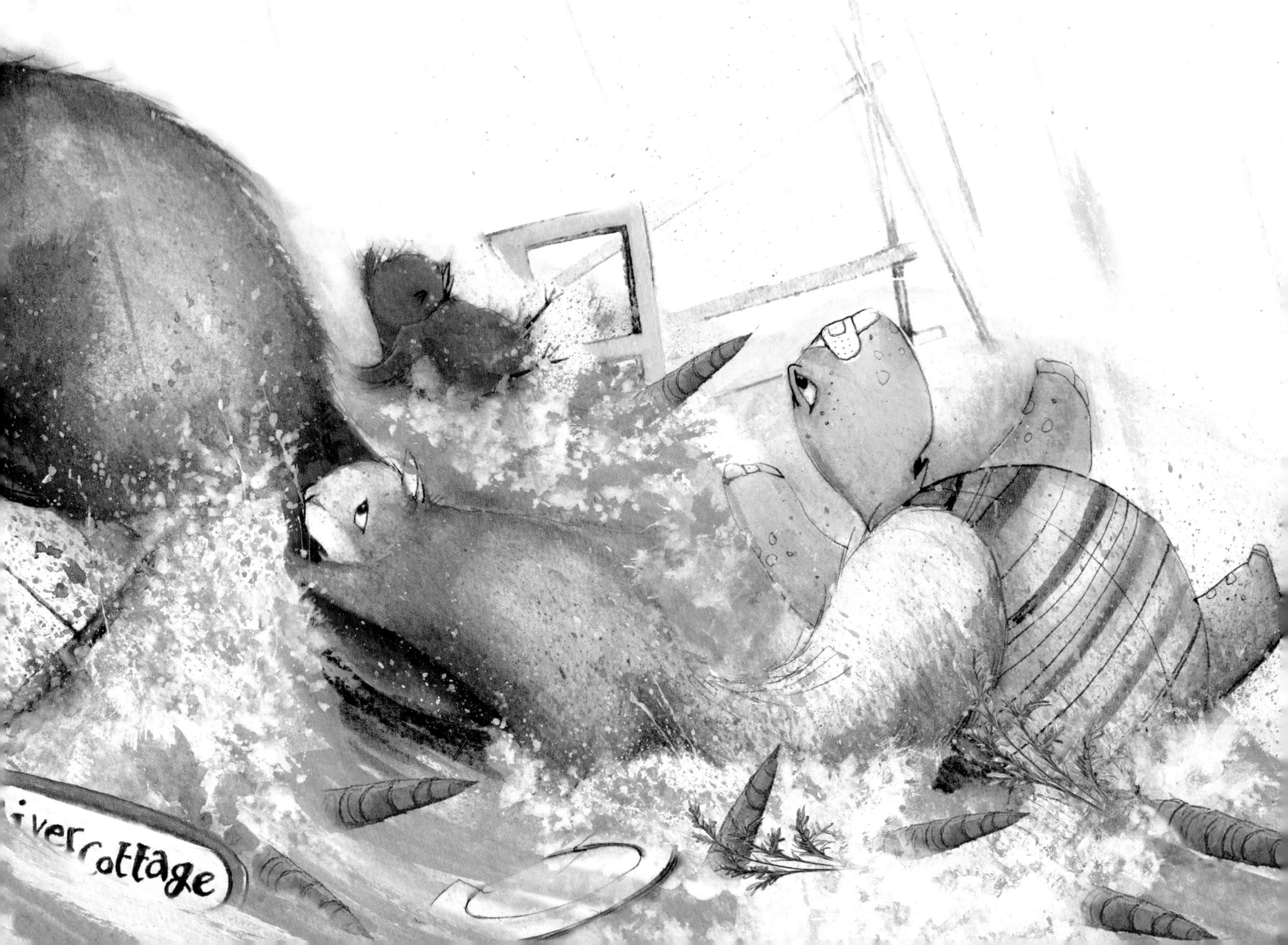

CRASH!

The friends groaned as they
swept up onto the riverbank.

Rabbit felt terrible. His friends were cold, tired, and homeless, and it was all his fault.

Even worse, Rabbit still had ALL of his carrots AND his house.

And that's when he realized there was only one thing to do . . .

...share everything with his friends! After all, carrots weren't for collecting – they were for

!PARTY!

SHARING!

And sharing made EVERYTHING better.

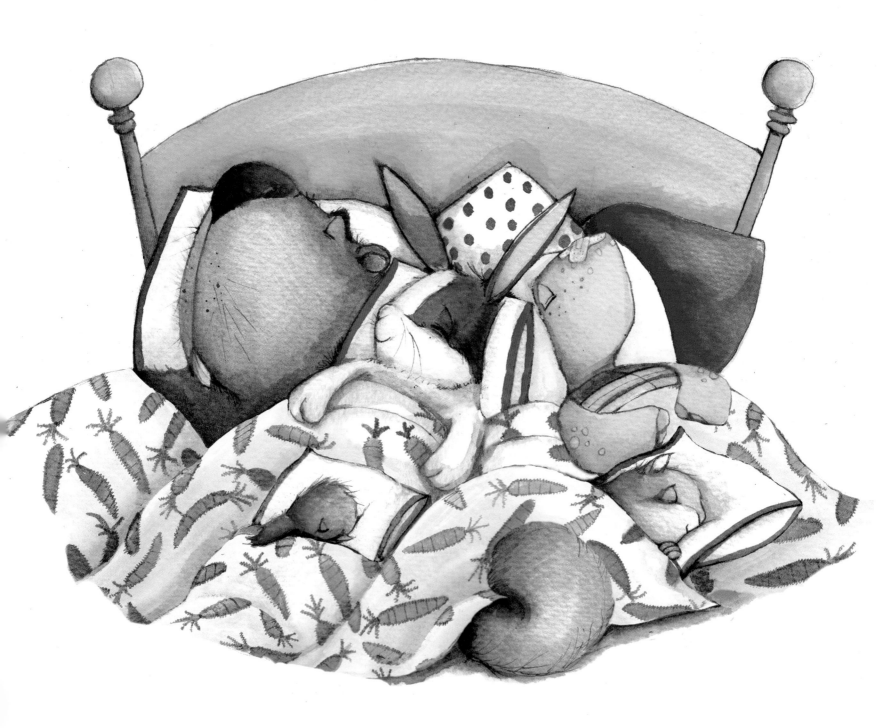